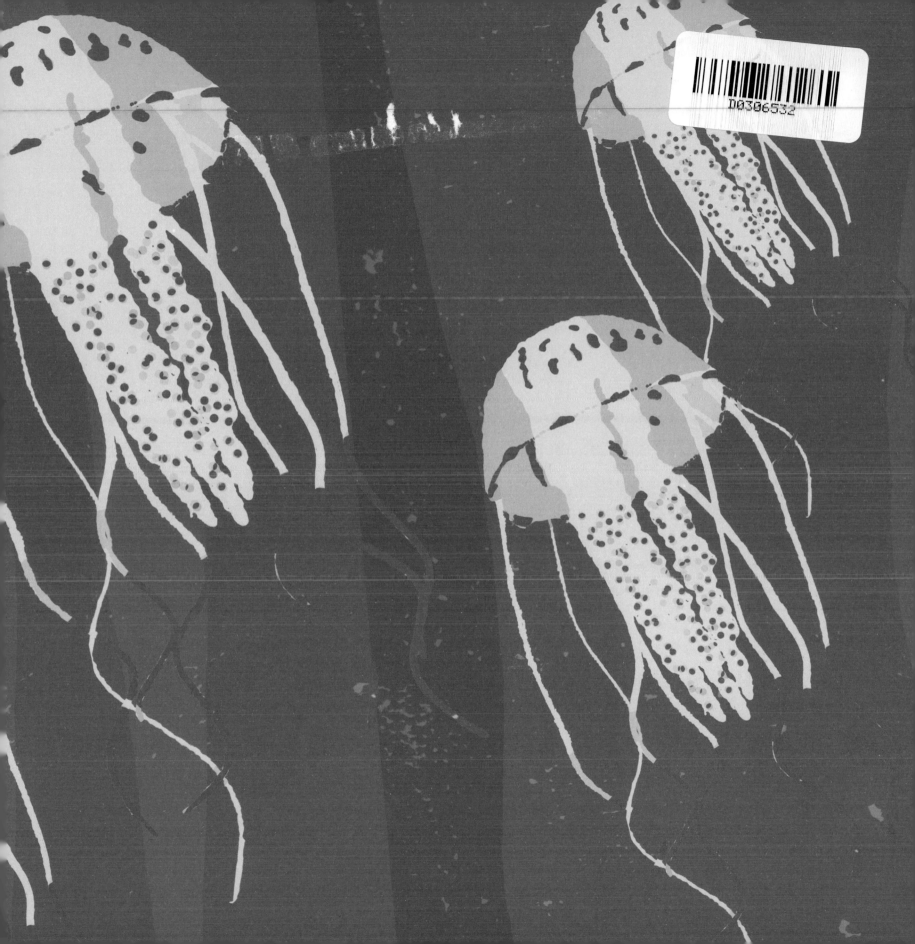

For Drew

First published in 2021 by Child's Play (International) Ltd
Ashworth Road, Bridgemead, Swindon SN5 7YD, UK

First published in USA in 2021 by Child's Play Inc
250 Minot Avenue, Auburn, Maine 04210

Distributed in Australia by Child's Play Australia Pty Ltd
Unit 10/20 Narabang Way, Belrose, Sydney, NSW 2085

Text and illustrations copyright © 2021 Julia Groves
The moral rights of the author/illustrator have been asserted

ISBN 978-1-78628-204-0
L120221CPL05212040

Printed in Heshan, China

1 3 5 7 9 10 8 6 4 2

A catalogue record of this book
is available from the British Library

www.childs-play.com

Protecting the Environment
This book has been printed using a waterless printing technique,
which offers the following environmental benefits:
No water is used in the process
No alcohol is involved, reducing greenhouse emissions
Less paper is used during set-up

I SEE THE SEA

Julia Groves

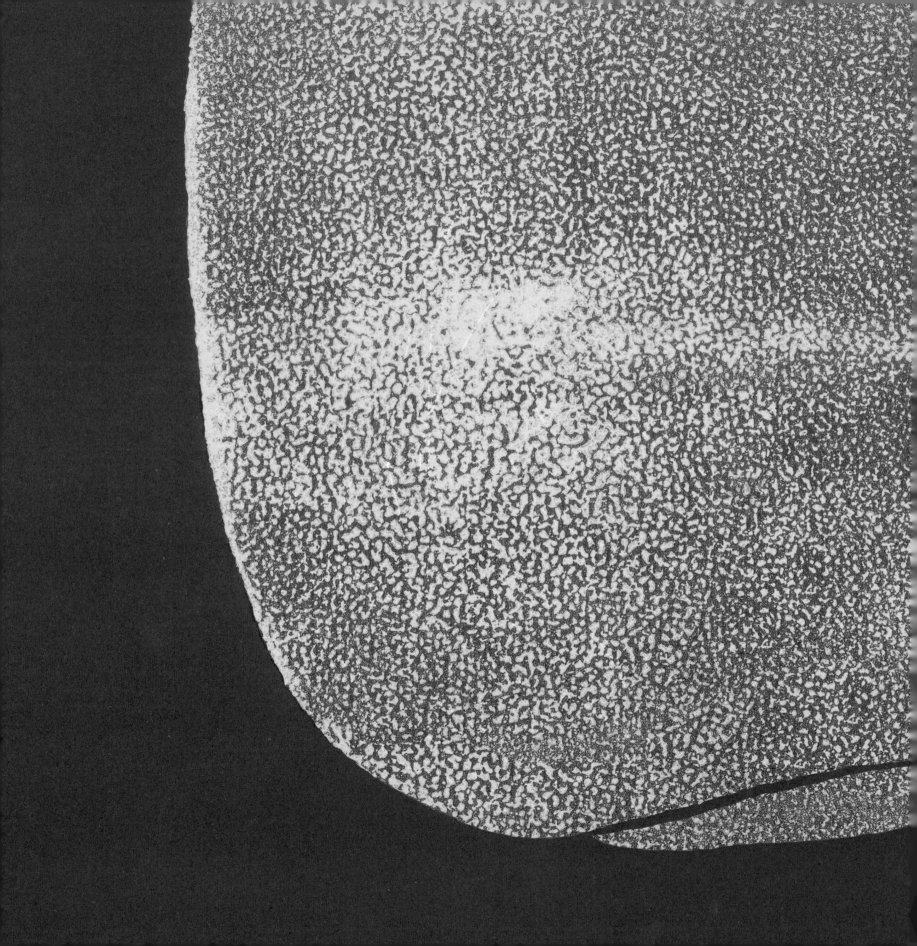

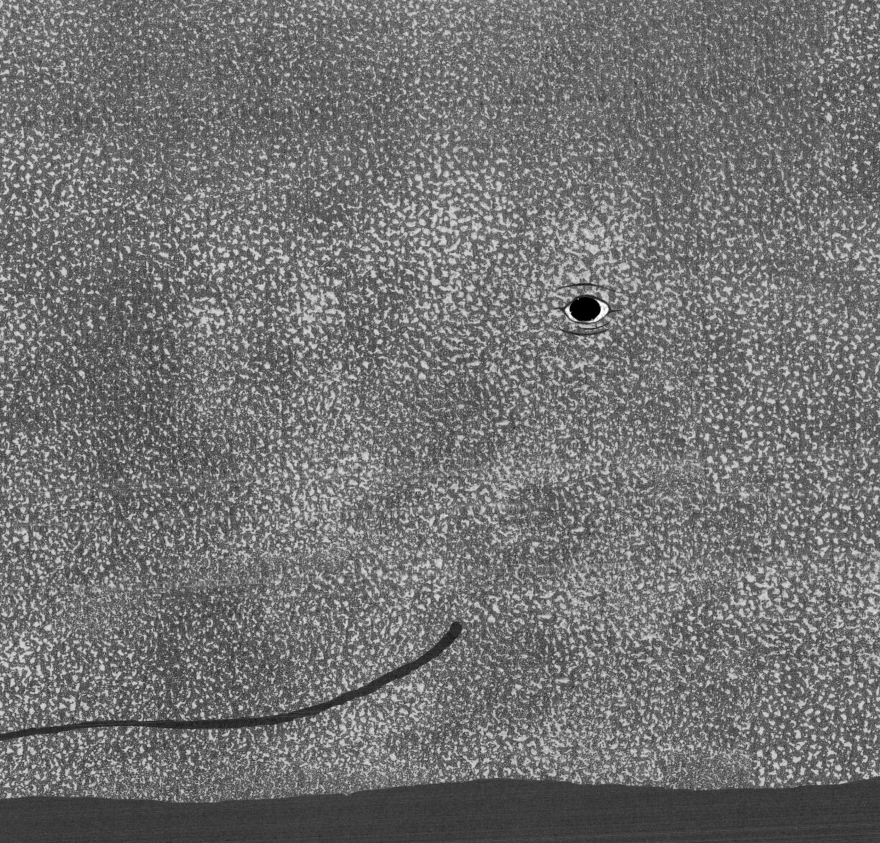

I SEE a dark shape gliding, majestic and serene.

I SEE a playful explosion, black and bright.

I SEE the knowing grasp, slow and swirling.

I SEE scattered light illuminating graceful wings.

I SEE a serene swimmer, alone in vast oceans.

I SEE night hunters
silently scouring
the ocean floor.

I SEE rasping teeth grazing on stony coral.

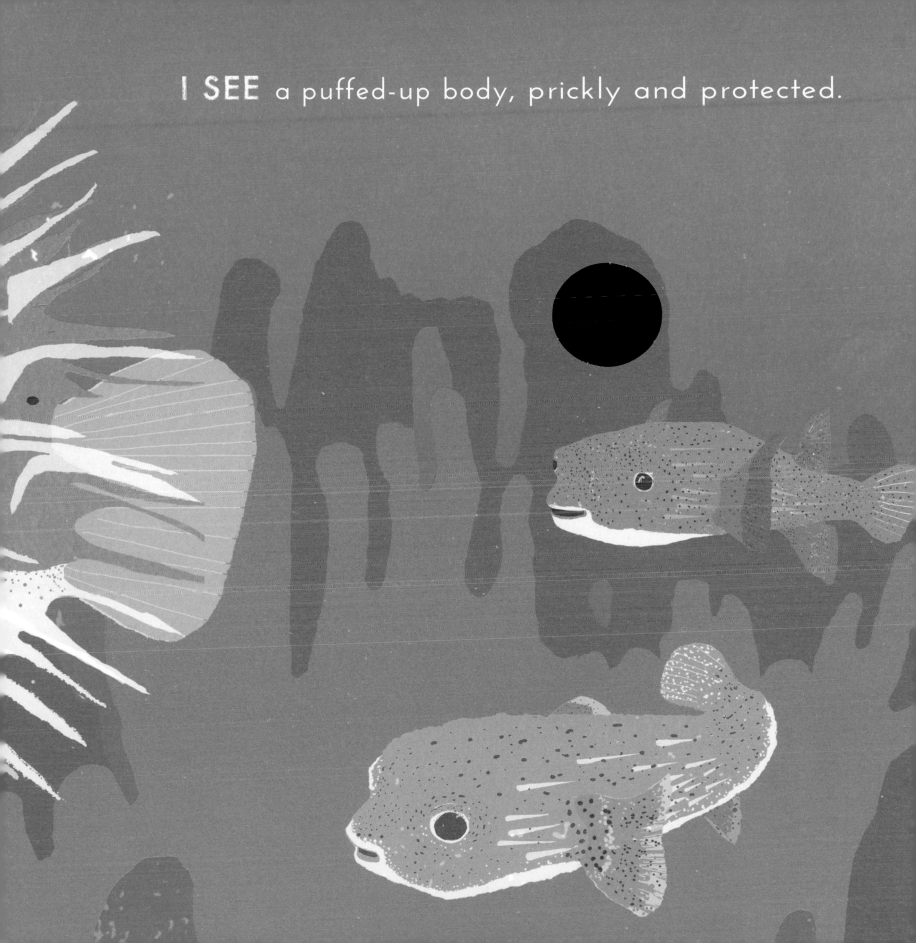

I SEE a puffed-up body, prickly and protected.

I SEE torpedo shapes jetting through open waters.

I SEE
shimmers
and flutters
clasping tight
for safety.

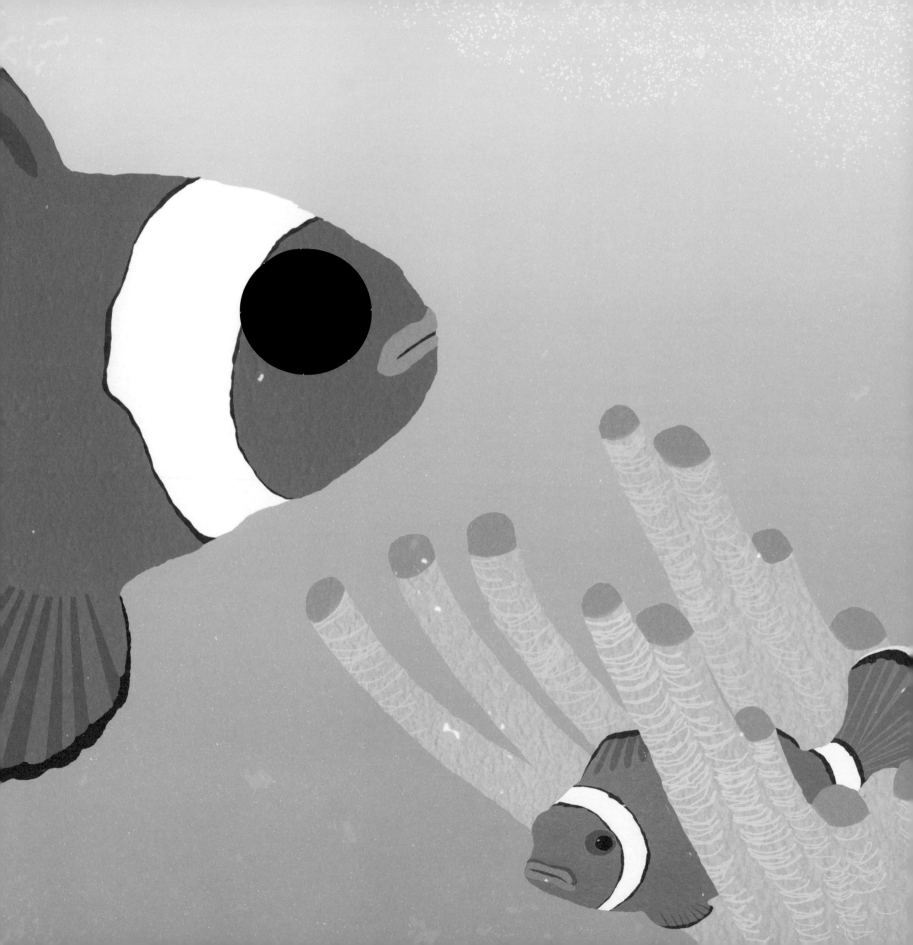

I SEE glints of orange
dancing between
waving tentacles.

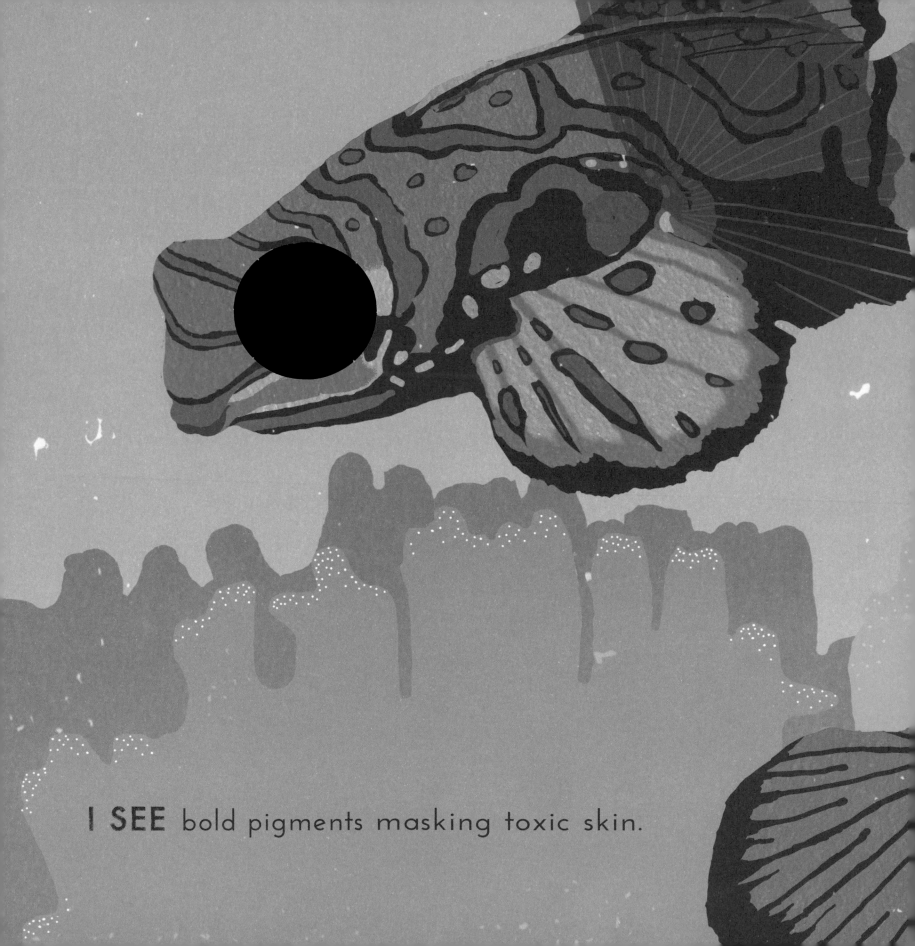

I SEE bold pigments masking toxic skin.

I SEE yellow flashes
darting between the fragile crusts.

WHO SEES
tiny plankton drifting silently?

Our Oceans and Seas

Formed about 3.3 billion years ago, the ocean covers about 70.9% of our planet's surface and holds about 1.34 billion km³ (321million mi³) of salt water – roughly 96.5% of all the water on Earth. Though one continuous body of water, it is divided into five main regions: Pacific, Atlantic, Indian, Arctic, and Southern. Smaller ocean regions are called seas, gulfs, and bays.

The ocean is vital to the health of our planet. It helps to keep Earth habitable by absorbing heat from the Sun and transporting it to the polar regions via ocean currents, regulating the climate and stopping places from getting too hot or cold. It also produces more than half the world's oxygen, absorbs about 50 times more carbon dioxide than our atmosphere, and is home to around 1 million known animal species, from the tiniest microorganisms to the world's largest living structure, the Great Barrier Reef, which is visible from space!

Today the ocean and the creatures that live there face many big challenges: climate change caused by human activity; pollution from plastic waste, noise and chemicals; habitat loss and destruction; overfishing; and acidification (caused by rising carbon dioxide levels in the Earth's atmosphere). The list is a long one, and all these things have an impact on the marine ecosystem. Heat stored in the oceans has increased, and this affects surface temperature, sea levels, and currents. Small changes in ocean conditions can have an enormous impact on the balance of wildlife, the reduction of species, their habitat, populations, and location. Reducing human impact on the ocean may not be able to repair the damage already done, but it will certainly make a difference to the future.

Sperm Whale (Physeter macrocephalus)

At up to 18m (60ft) long, sperm whales are the biggest of the toothed whales and have the largest brain of any creature on Earth. Their diet consists mainly of fish and squid – about 1 metric ton every day! Adults can dive to depths of up to 1,000m (3,280ft) in search of food, and hold their breath for as long as 90 minutes before returning to the surface. Using echolocation to find prey, they make a series of 'clicks' as loud as 230 decibels – louder than a space shuttle launch! When these sounds hit an object, they bounce back, relaying information about the object's location, size, and shape. These marine mammals live in groups of about 15, called pods, made up mainly of females and their calves. Males roam the ocean alone or move between pods. Sperm whales are now endangered, due to threats from chemical and noise pollution, marine debris, and climate change.

Killer Whale (Orcinus orca)

These highly intelligent marine mammals are not whales but the largest members of the dolphin family, with males growing up to 8m (26ft) long. They are found in all the world's oceans and sit at the top of the food chain, with no natural predators. Also known as orcas, they live and hunt in groups of up to 40, called pods, and feed on a wide range of creatures, including fish, seabirds, seals, squid, and even whales. They identify their prey using echolocation, and work together as a team to catch it, employing a variety of ingenious hunting techniques. They communicate via a wide range of sounds particular to their group – the pod's own 'language' – and have a sophisticated social structure similar to that of apes. This strong family culture and their drive to hunt and swim up to 70km (40mi) per day have led to controversy over keeping them in captivity, where an orca's natural life span of 70 years can be halved.

Giant Pacific Octopus
(Enteroctopus dofleini)

Elusive and shy, these incredible creatures live in the cold waters of the coastal north Pacific at depths of up to 2,000m (6,500ft) and are thought to be the world's largest species of octopus. The biggest specimen ever found was more than 9m (30ft) across, but they usually measure about half this size. With enormous bulging heads, they are masters of disguise, using pigment cells in their skin to change their markings to blend in with the surroundings. This camouflage technique is perfect for hunting prey. Octopuses wait, then grab their victims – snails, clams, scallops, shrimp, lobsters, and fish – with their eight arms, before crunching them with their hard beak. Known to be extremely intelligent, octopuses have been filmed escaping from tanks in captivity and squirting water at people who annoy them! Though not currently classified as under threat, acidification of the ocean is reducing these creatures' food sources.

Spotted Eagle Ray (Aetobatus narinari)

These incredible predators are found in the shallow coastal waters of tropical regions around the world, at depths down to 80m (260ft). The skeleton of their flattened body is made of cartilage rather than bone, and they can reach widths of more than 3m (11ft) when fully grown. They are very fast swimmers, flapping their large wing-like fins to 'fly' through the ocean, and can leap out of the water and across its surface. Their beak-like snout is used to dig up prey, such as small fish, octopuses, molluscs, crabs, and lobsters from the seabed, before they crack open any tough shells with their extra-hard teeth and devour the meal. They are equipped with venomous, barbed spines at the base of their whip-like tail, which they lash out at predators. They often fall prey to sharks, but the main threat to these rays' existence is not ocean predators, but pollution, overfishing, and excessive collecting for the aquarium trade.

Leatherback Sea Turtle
(Dermochelys coriacea)

Leatherbacks are the largest turtles on Earth and one of the most endangered creatures on the planet. More than 2m (7ft) long when mature, their streamlined body and ridged shell are designed to help them power through the water, propelled by huge flippers up to 2.7m (9ft) in length. The species is found in all subtropical and tropical oceans, with a range that extends into the Arctic Circle. Though females can lay more than 100 eggs in a clutch, only 6% of infants will survive their first year. Most are eaten by predators or become disorientated by the light from human settlements after hatching and cannot find their way to the ocean. Taking many years to mature, this species is vulnerable to even small increases in the death rate of youngsters and adults. Turtles mainly eat jellyfish and often mistake floating plastic waste in the ocean for food. Up to a third of leatherbacks may now have plastic in their stomachs.

European Lobster (Homarus gammarus)

European lobsters begin life as tiny eggs, which females protect under their tail for 10 to 11 months, held in place by a natural glue they produce. Once hatched, the larvae float to the surface to dine on plankton for about 10 weeks. Although females may lay 15,000 eggs at a time, most are eaten by predators at this larval stage. Survivors burrow into the sediment on the ocean bed for two years until they mature, forming a hard external skeleton called an exoskeleton. Adult lobsters can live for 70 years and may grow up to 60cm (24in). In order to reach this size, they must shed their exoskeleton several times a year when young, and once every few years when adult. During this process, the shell splits open between the tail and the body, and lobsters flex to wriggle out backwards. It takes two weeks for a new exoskeleton to form and harden, and at this stage, they are easy targets for predators.

Stoplight Parrotfish (*Sparisoma viride*)

Found in shallow tropical and subtropical reefs around the world, these blunt-faced, elongated fish change pattern and hue throughout the three different phases of their life. They are named for the yellow spot on their pectoral fin, which appears in the final phase. A fully grown male can grow up to 60cm (24in) long and will fight for territory. Parrotfish graze on coral, using their beak-like mouth, containing more than 1,000 super-hard teeth arranged in rows, to break off chunks. Further inside the mouth, at the back of the throat, are more teeth. These grind up the coral, releasing the nutritious algae that live inside. The waste from this process is released from the fish's rear end forms the white sand found on tropical beaches. Most parrotfish start life as females, but they are able to change gender back and forth in response to an imbalance between breeding males and females.

Spot-Fin Porcupinefish
(*Diodon hystrix*)

Spot-fin porcupinefish are nocturnal, solitary fish found in all the tropical and subtropical oceans of the world, where they seek food and shelter in rocky reefs, under ledges, and in caves. They have large protruding eyes, a wide flattened mouth and can grow up to 90cm (3ft) in length. Their brown spotted skin is covered with long, sharp spines, which are folded back against the body. When under attack, porcupinefish inflate themselves to look bigger by swallowing water and raising their spines for protection. If this doesn't act as a deterrent, some organs of their body also contain a powerful poison that can kill a predator (including humans) if eaten. It is most toxic before and during spawning. Hard-shelled sea creatures, such as large sea urchins, lobsters, and crabs, make up most of their diet. Rubbery lips protect them from broken shells, while they crush their prey with super-strong jaws and teeth that are fused together.

Caribbean Reef Squid
(*Sepioteuthis sepioidea*)

Along with other cephalopods, such as the octopuses and cuttlefish, Caribbean reef squid are believed by scientists to be capable of dreaming. Evidence for this is found in their ability to change shades and skin pattern when sleeping – something they normally do in response to a threat or to indicate a mood change. They are usually found in shallow coral reefs up to 8m (26ft) beneath the surface, but are also known to show a preference for specific locations, depending on the time of day and even how old they are. Some have been spotted at depths of 100m (325ft) or more. Their 30cm-long torpedo-shaped body has rippling fins down the sides to help them swim. Two tentacles are used to strike out and catch their prey of small fish and shrimps, and eight arms are used to hold on to prey and place it in the squid's mouth. To escape predators, squid produce a cloud of dark ink in the water to confuse their attackers.

Spiny Seahorse (*Hippocampus histrix*)

With their horse-like head and wriggling tail, these tiny fish are completely covered in thorns. Their long toothless snout is used to search in crevices for prey and works like a hoover to suck up food. Their prehensile tail can grip on to seaweed, anchoring seahorses in ocean currents to avoid being swept away. When hunting for food, they rely on their eyesight and are able to move each eye independently. They eat tiny crustaceans, such as shrimp. Adults can consume as many as 50 shrimp a day, digesting their meal whole with the help of bile. This is the only species where males become pregnant and give birth to live young. Females transfer their eggs to the males' pouch and they self-fertilise them. When the pups are fully grown, they are expelled from the males' pouch. These unique creatures are now under threat from Chinese medicine, the pet trade, overfishing, and habitat destruction.

False Percula Clownfish
(*Amphiprion ocellaris*)

False percula clownfish live in sea anemones in the lagoons and reefs off the coast of Western Australia and Southeast Asia. Clownfish are coated with a mucus that helps them to build up immunity, so they are not harmed by the painful sting of anemone tentacles. In turn, the fish eat parasites that live on their hosts, helping the anemones to stay healthy. This is called a symbiotic relationship. Most clownfish are bright orange, with three white bands outlined in black across their body; though this can vary, depending on where in the world the fish are found. A highly territorial species, they live in small groups and have a strong social hierarchy, communicating by making popping and clicking noises. Groups are made up of one female, the rest being male. The dominant male breeds with the female. If the female dies, the dominant male changes into a female and finds a new mate.

Mandarinfish (*Synchiropus splendidus*)

With their gorgeous markings and bright rainbow pigments, these little fish are aptly named after the beautiful silk robes of mandarins, or scholars, in Imperial China. But their appearance is more than just decorative – it also acts as a warning to predators. Their skin secretes a smelly, bad-tasting mucus and has a layer of special cells that release toxins to repel attackers. Their bright appearance also helps when females gather in groups on the reef, looking for a mate. The males, which grow up to 6cm (2½in) long, do a courtship dance to impress the females, who then choose the biggest, strongest, most attractive fish to mate with. Successful males can mate with several females in one night. Mandarinfish are found in tropical waters in much of the western Pacific. They live on the bottom of the ocean at depths of up to 18m (60ft), using their large pelvic fins to 'walk' around on the seabed.

Yellow Tang (*Zebrasoma flavescens*)

Tang fish are so named for the small white scalpel or spine, known as a tang, on the side of their body, just near the tail, which they use to warn off predators and competitors for food or territory. It is the only part of their body that is not yellow, and males and females are hard to tell apart, except during courtship. Commonly found alone or in small groups, they live in the shallow reefs of the Pacific, west of Hawaii and east of Japan. During the day they graze on the coral reefs with their snout-shaped mouths, which makes it easier for them to pick off algae and seaweed. Though they appear bright yellow to the human eye, the tangs blend in with their coral habitat, helping them to hide from predators. Popular as an aquarium fish, the species benefits from the Marine Protected Areas around Hawaii, which allow populations to thrive by protecting them against overfishing.

Plankton

These microscopic organisms play one of the most important roles in the ocean ecosystem, providing vital food for creatures big and small, from shrimps to whales. Rarely visible to the human eye, most drift on the currents, though some can swim. They can be classified into two groups: phytoplankton (plants), and zooplankton (animals). Like all plants, phytoplankton harness energy from the sun to create sugar, which they need to survive. Through this process, called photosynthesis, they are the world's biggest producers of oxygen. Zooplankton include the young of jellyfish, fish, and other microscopic animals, such as krill and seasnails. During the day they drift into deep water to avoid predators; at night they float to the surface and feed on phytoplankton. All plankton are sensitive to their environment, and even small changes in temperature, nutrients, and acidity can have an impact.

Our Endangered Oceans

Overfishing

This is the biggest threat to the world's oceans. By catching fish faster than stocks can replenish, some fishing practices cause depletion and even the extinction of some species. Fewer than 5% of our oceans are protected against commercial fishing, and vessels now spend months at sea, returning with hugely valuable catches. However, it has been calculated that 40% of the total global catch is accidental and unwanted, and is simply thrown back into the water, dead or injured.

YOU CAN HELP by eating less seafood. If you do eat fish, check that it has been sustainably sourced. A good place to start is to check that is has the MSC label. Try to support calls for better laws and greater protection for the world's stocks of fish and seafood.

Plastic Pollution

Almost 50% of plastic pollution comes from the fishing industry, with tons of nets, lines, hooks, pots, and traps discarded every year. Other items finishing up in our oceans include face wipes and sanitary products containing plastic flushed down the toilet, and plastic microfibres released from our clothes when we wash them, which are too small to be filtered out of waste water. Illegal dumping of waste adds huge amounts of plastic to the ocean. However careful we are, plastic has a habit of ending up in the ocean. It's very light, therefore easily blown around into drains and rivers that carry it down to the sea. Unlike other materials, plastic does not degrade, it simply breaks down into smaller and smaller particles. Tiny beads of broken-down plastic contain and absorb pollutants, which find their way into the ocean. These microfibres are ingested by marine creatures, while larger items are mistaken for food, and can also entangle and trap fish and animals.

YOU CAN HELP by reducing the number of single-use plastic items you buy, and by recycling plastic as much as possible. Use your own non-plastic shopping bags, and try not to buy plastic-wrapped food. Reuse items whenever you can, never flush items that contain plastic down the toilet, and don't throw your gum on the ground. If you live near the coast, help regularly with a local beach clean-up.

Chemical Pollution

Harmful chemicals in cleaning products get washed down the drain and end up in the ocean. Chemicals used in the soil and on farmers' crops also end up in the water system. These chemicals can react in water, causing oxygen levels to drop.

YOU CAN HELP prevent this by eating organic food, grown without using such chemicals. The best cleaning products to use are biodegradable – this means they break down into natural elements that don't harm the environment.

Light Pollution

More than half the world's cities are close to water. As their populations increase, the ocean environment is being affected more and more by human activity. Light pollution can affect the lives of many ocean species. Bright lights from buildings, for example, mean that animals that normally hunt during the day can now also hunt throughout the night, but this means there are no safe times for their prey.

YOU CAN HELP by using as few outdoor lights as possible, and by making sure they are shielded and aimed downwards. Turn off lights when they are not needed, and use curtains, drapes, and blinds when it's dark.

Transport Pollution

Road vehicles transport goods around the world and contribute carbon emissions to the atmosphere, as well as plastic pollution from rubber treads. Many of the items we buy have been transported across oceans on huge ships. Commercial shipping, military sonar, and oil exploration all create noise that ocean creatures find extremely disruptive. These include whales and dolphins, which travel huge distances while using their delicate hearing to communicate, navigate, find food, and avoid predators.

YOU CAN HELP by shopping locally and buying products that are made and grown nearby. Walk or cycle to the shops and school whenever you can. Use public transport or car share if you need to make a longer journey. Reduce your purchasing, as every item you buy has an impact on the environment.

Energy Pollution

Greenhouse gases are created by burning fossil fuels, such as coal, crude oil, and natural gas. Fossil fuels are used to provide electricity and heat, and to power motorcars, trucks, ships, trains, and planes. Fossil fuels produce large quantities of carbon dioxide when burned, and these emissions trap heat in the atmosphere, leading to climate change. The ocean absorbs most of the excess heat from these emissions, resulting in rising ocean levels and temperatures, higher acidity, and lower oxygen levels. Coral reefs, for example, are being 'bleached' by climate change and are being destroyed, along with the many species that depend on them.

YOU CAN HELP by using less energy at home, and by making fewer car journeys. Planting trees reduces greenhouse gases by removing carbon dioxide from the atmosphere and releasing oxygen.

There are other ways **YOU CAN HELP**. Try eating less meat, as most meat production creates huge amounts of greenhouse gases. Plan your meals to reduce wastage. Disposing of food waste in landfill sites produces large amounts of methane, which adds to global warming. You may have space to grow some of your own food, which can be fun and really good for the environment. It's really about using less and choosing wisely.

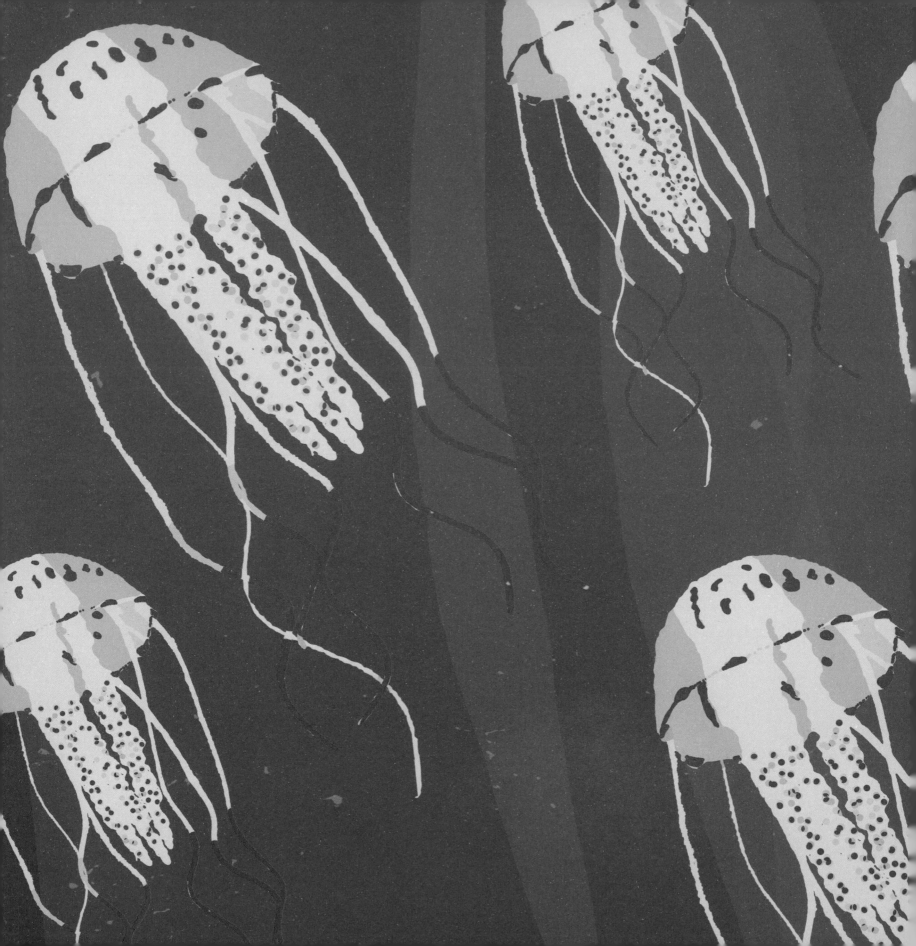